THIS BOOK BELONGS TO

children's choice®

 A Children's Choice® Book Club Edition from Macmillan Book Clubs, Inc.

Arlene Dubanevich

PIG WILLIAM

Bradbury Press   New York

Bradbury Press
An Affiliate of Macmillan, Inc.
866 Third Avenue, New York, N.Y. 10022
Collier Macmillan Canada, Inc.
Manufactured in the United States of America
10 9 8 7 6 5 4 3 2
The text of this book is hand-lettered by the artist.
The illustrations are four-color pre-separated drawings, reproduced in line and halftone.
Library of Congress Cataloging in Publication Data:
    Dubanevich, Arlene. Pig William.
    Summary: Always a dawdler, Pig William misses his ride to the school picnic but in a sudden turn of
events the picnic comes to him.
    1. Children's stories, American.   [1. Pigs — Fiction.   2. Picnicking — Fiction]   I. Title
PZ7.D8492Pi   1985   [E]   85-5776
ISBN 0-02-733200-4

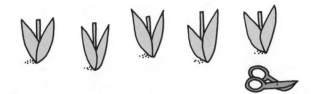